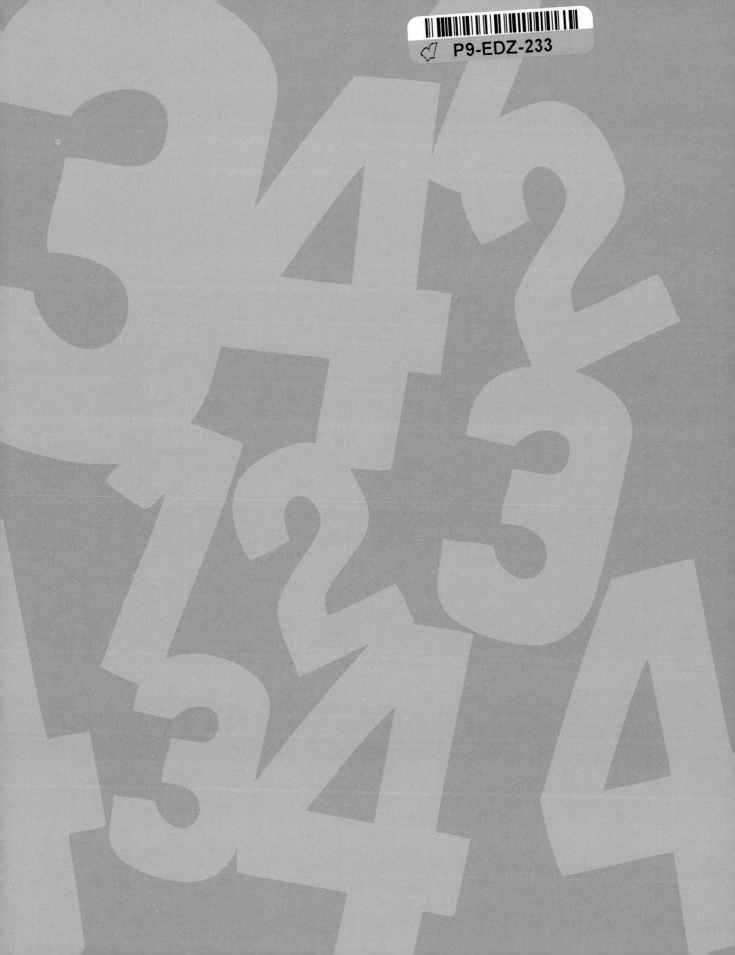

'S NUMBER THOUGHTS

A STORY ABOUT OCD

Natalie Rompella

illustrated by Alessia Girasole

Albert Whitman & Company
Chicago, Illinois

"I'm having a mini golf birthday party on Saturday!" Cora told Malik and Jason.

One, two, three, four. One, two, three, four...Malik's foot tapped the floor.

"It'll be so fun!" Cora bounced in her seat. "The winner gets to come back and play another round of mini golf for free."

"I can't wait!" Jason said.

One, two, three, four. One, two, three, four...Malik patted his lunch bag.

Malik hoped his Number Thoughts would let him play.

Malik's Number Thoughts had started last year. They made him count everything he did. If he did not count exactly to four, Malik felt scared and worried. When he walked to school or up any stairs, he felt relieved if he finished on his fourth step. He felt frustrated if he didn't and had to start over.

Sometimes it took him many tries.

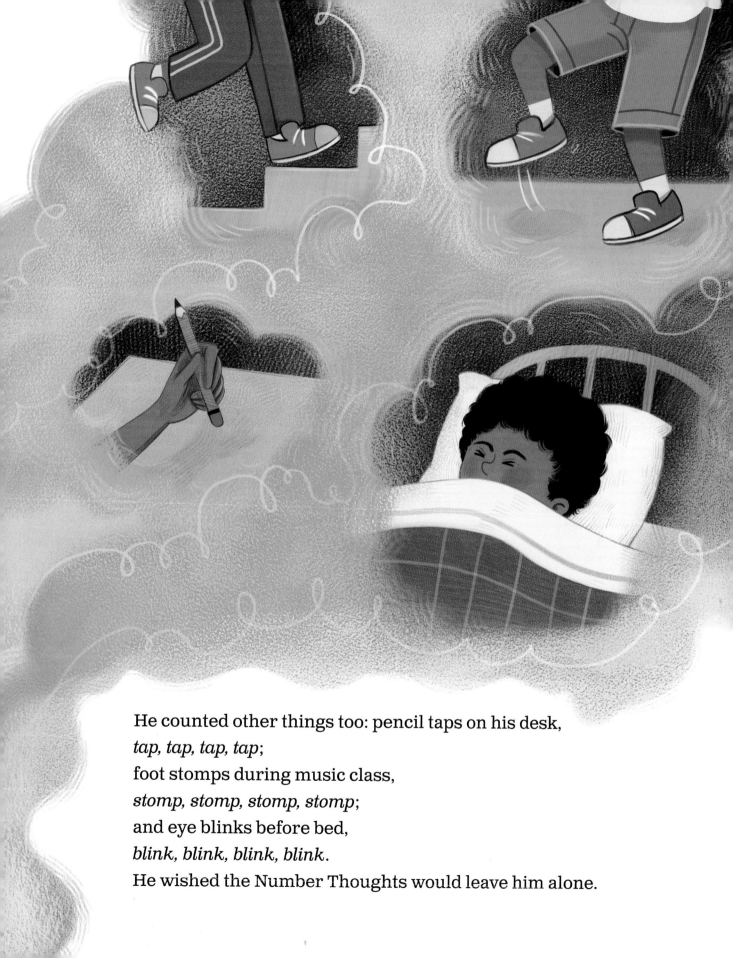

He counted other things too: pencil taps on his desk,
tap, tap, tap, tap;
foot stomps during music class,
stomp, stomp, stomp, stomp;
and eye blinks before bed,
blink, blink, blink, blink.
He wished the Number Thoughts would leave him alone.

When Malik got home from school, he told his dad about the party.

"I really want to go, but I'm worried about my Number Thoughts," Malik said.

"I think it would be great for you to play mini golf. You see Dr. Thomas tonight. She can help you get ready."

Dr. Thomas was a special doctor. She helped kids whose thoughts sometimes got stuck and caused them to repeat a task, such as washing their hands or arranging toys a certain way.

She was helping Malik with his Number Thoughts.

"What if my Number Thoughts take over?" Malik asked.

"If that happens, do what we've practiced to make it easier to ignore them," said Dr. Thomas. "Take slow, deep breaths. Look around. Notice what you see, touch, hear, smell, and taste."

Malik nodded.

"I know some days are better than others, but practice helps," Dr. Thomas said. "Each time you overcome your Number Thoughts, you get better at beating them."

Malik remembered how awful he felt the first time he got to school on a third step. Now it didn't feel so bad.

"But how can I practice mini golf before the party?"

Dr. Thomas smiled. "I have an idea."

When Malik got home from school the next day,
his dad had a surprise.

"You can make your own mini golf course!" his dad said.

"Can Jason help?" Malik asked.

Malik and Jason worked on their mini golf course for hours.

"Let's try it!" Jason said.

Malik looked at the course.

One part of his brain told him, *You must get the ball in on the fourth stroke.*

Another part of his brain told him, *You should go for a hole-in-two.*

Which would win?

Malik felt his heart *beat, beat, beat, beating*.

"You can do it," Jason said.

Malik hit the ball.

It flew through the box and up the ramp, then bounced off the plant.

"Wow! Great shot!" Jason said. He hit his ball. It rolled under the couch.

Thump, thump, thump, thump, Malik rapped his club on the floor. He could probably get the ball into the hole on the next shot. But his brain wanted him to miss. Twice.

No, he told his brain. *Don't listen to the Number Thoughts.*

He took slow, deep breaths. He knew he'd feel awful if he didn't end on a four, but that after a while, he'd feel better.

He gently tapped the ball…

In it went.

"Great putt!" Jason said.

Malik smiled, but his stomach churned.

His dad peeked in the room. "How are you doing?"

"Malik just made a hole-in-two!" Jason told him.

"That's great! How do you feel?" his dad asked.

Malik couldn't answer. He was trying too hard not to cry.

His dad patted his shoulder. It was their secret way of reminding Malik to take deep breaths and use his senses.

Malik breathed slowly. He noticed his dad's T-shirt, the *drip-drip* sound of the coffee maker, and the smell of chicken in the oven.

"Let's try the next one," he said.

On the day of Cora's party, Malik was worried. What if he didn't get the ball in the hole in exactly four strokes? Would he feel like bursting from the urge to obey his Number Thoughts? What if he *did* listen to them? Would the other kids laugh at him?

"We're sure to win after all our practicing," Jason told Malik.
If only Malik didn't have to worry so much about his
Number Thoughts.

Malik stepped onto the first putting green. He set down his ball and hit it. *Whack*. The ball rolled back to the beginning of the course. Stroke one.

He hit the ball again. *Whack*. It stopped inches from the hole. Stroke two.

"Just tap it in," Jason said.

One, two, three, four, the numbers chanted in Malik's head.

One, two, three—no. He wasn't going to let the Number Thoughts win.

He lined up his club.

Tap.

Plop. The ball dropped in.

He took slow, deep breaths in through his nose and out through his mouth. He pretended he was blowing the Number Thoughts away.

On the next hole, he got another three. And then a four. Then a two. Each hole made him feel jittery, but he kept on going.

They reached the final hole. Everyone else had finished.
"If you get a score of three or lower, you'll win," Jason said.
That meant Malik couldn't get a four.

Malik examined the obstacles. He had a good chance of getting close to the hole on the first try. Or he could get a four and make his Number Thoughts happy.

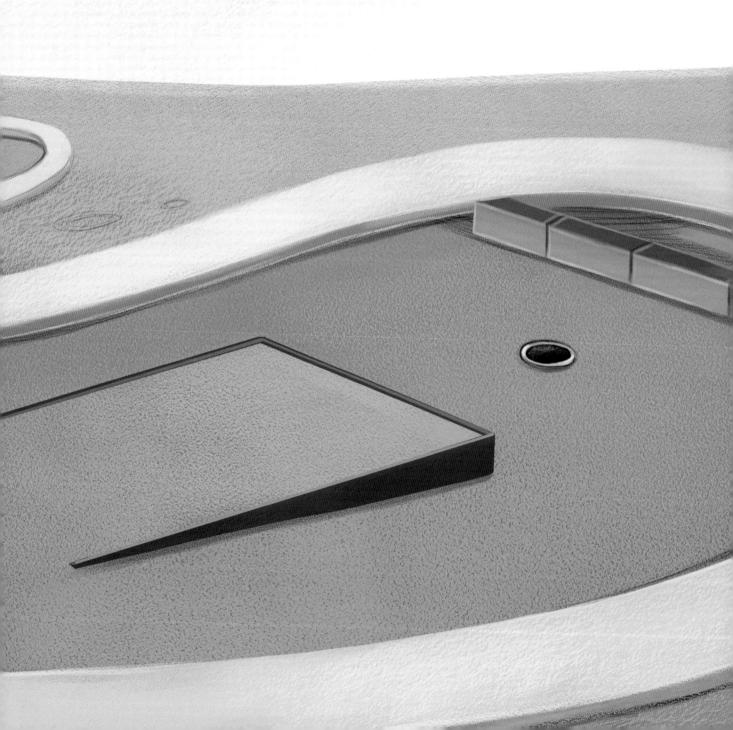

Tap, tap, tap, tap. His fingers drummed on his leg.

Malik looked at Jason. He listened to the sound of someone hitting a ball nearby. He smelled pizza in the air.

He put his hands around the club, breathed in through his nose...
out through his mouth, and *whack*.
The ball went up the ramp.
It hit the back wall...

and rolled into the hole.

"A hole in one!" Jason shouted. "You won! We get to come back and play again!"

Malik smiled. Winning against the Number Thoughts felt good.

WHAT IS OCD?

Malik has a condition called obsessive-compulsive disorder (OCD). It causes a person to think uncontrollably about something (to obsess) and then perform a repeated action to make the thoughts go away (a compulsion). Malik feels the need to count and do things in sets of four.

Other kinds of OCD include uncontrollable thoughts or feelings of being dirty or contaminated and needing to wash hands repeatedly, of having left something turned on and needing to check it repeatedly, of needing to arrange or touch objects in a particular way, and of having done something wrong and needing to pray just the right way.

Often someone will have more than one form of OCD, such as both needing to wash and needing to check that objects are turned off. According to the International OCD Foundation, OCD affects about one in two hundred children in the United States.

Malik goes to a therapist who helps with his unwanted thoughts and actions by guiding him through exposure and response prevention therapy (ERP). This means practicing things that trigger OCD (the exposure) while not giving in to the urge to do the compulsive action (the response prevention). Malik also learns ways to work through his anxiety (feelings of nervousness and fear), including taking deep breaths and using his five senses. These techniques trigger a calming response in the nervous system that cues the body to relax. A pediatrician or school counselor can assist in finding a therapist who treats OCD.

To learn more about OCD, go to iocdf.org or beyondocd.org.

Five Senses Mindfulness Exercise

Look around and notice...

- five things you can see
- four things you can touch
- three things you can hear
- two things you can smell
- one thing you can taste

To the real Jason—who really is a supportive friend—NR

To all children who have felt "different"—AG

Library of Congress Cataloging-in-Publication data is on file with the publisher.
Text copyright © 2022 by Natalie Rompella
Illustrations copyright © 2022 by Albert Whitman & Company
Illustrations by Alessia Girasole
First published in the United States of America in 2022 by Albert Whitman & Company
ISBN 978-0-8075-4950-6 (hardcover)
ISBN 978-0-8075-4951-3 (ebook)
Printed in China
10 9 8 7 6 5 4 3 2 1 WKT 26 25 24 23 22

Design by Tim Palin Creative

For more information about Albert Whitman & Company,
visit our website at www.albertwhitman.com.

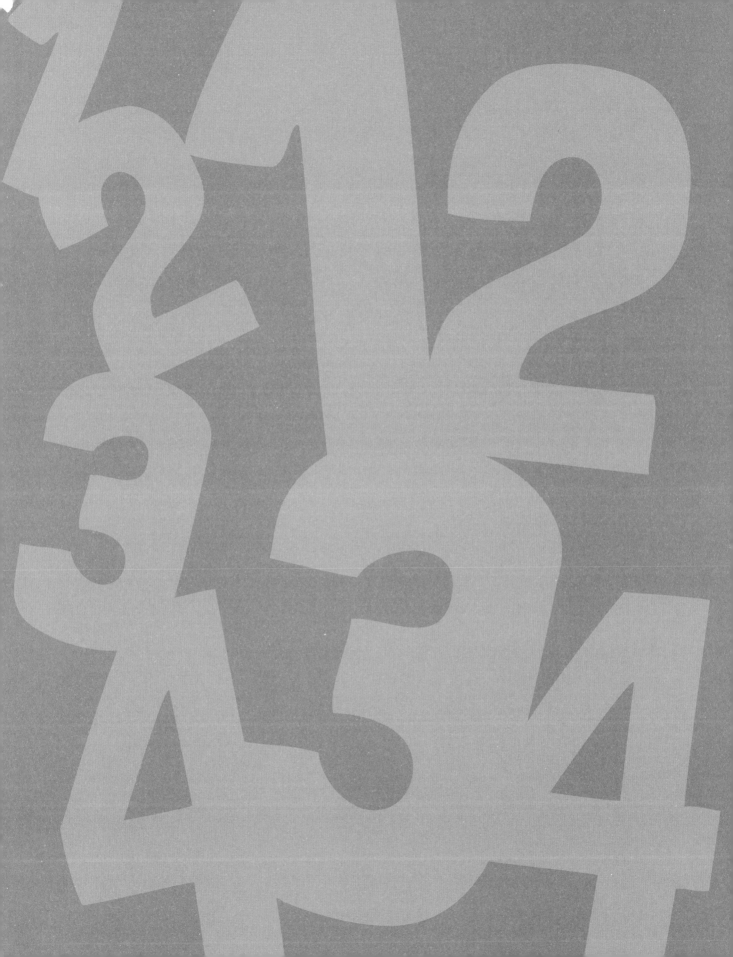